MW01107781

GEOFF AND THE RIDE OF HIS LIFE

Written by
LOUISE RENWICK

Illustrated by
ADELINE KO

All monkeys misbehave,
none more so than little gibbons.

Imagine the cheekiest of cheeky
monkeys, multiply that by the
biggest number of bananas
that you can think of, and you'd get...

Geoff.

Like most
mischief-makers,
Geoff grew up
causing his parents
no end of trouble.

Whenever
Mummy Gibbon
called, "Bed time!"
Geoff would swing
past her waving his
pyjamas around his
head, hooting,

"Catch me if you can!"

When he wasn't in school or making mischief at home, Geoff spent his time doing what gibbons love to do most: climbing high, swinging through the trees, chit-chatting with his buddies, and of course, eating bananas.

But as time went by, Geoff began to **wonder** what lay outside his jungle home. "I want to do *more* than swing in the trees, Mum. I'm *bored* of having no new tricks up my sleeve."

Luckily, Mummy Gibbon had a trick of her own up her sleeve.

She bought Geoff the perfect gift for his birthday.

"**Chin up!**" she said, and kissed him on the forehead as he buckled on his shiny new helmet.

"Yippeee!"
whooped Geoff,
and off he whizzed.

Cycling away from his home, Geoff weaved over rivers filled with fierce crocodiles and spiralled through mountains full of strange birds...

Each road brought new friends who pedalled alongside him, urging him to keep his hairy little legs spinning.

A few weeks into his journey,
Geoff met the Gibbon King.
When the King saw how
FIT and **STRONG** Geoff was,
he invited him to train for
an important event.

"I'm going to send you to a race
in *Beijing*," he hooted.

"All the best
cyclists in the
world will
be there!"

Geoff trained hard.

Whenever he wasn't cycling, he was sleeping, and when he wasn't sleeping, he was *cycling*.

No more staying out late with friends, no more birthday parties and celebrations. Geoff's jungle buddies hardly *ever* saw him.

However, as the months went by, Geoff became *e x h a u s t e d !*

He decided it was about time he gave his legs a well-earned rest.

So he slung a small bag over his shoulder and jumped onto a ferry.

Very soon, Geoff found himself on the shore of a beautiful island filled with **butterflies** and plenty of bananas.

It felt like *paradise.*

But that night, as he gazed at the moon and breathed in the sea air, a tear filled his eye. The island's fresh air felt good, but he missed laughing and joking with his friends.

Geoff longed to be swinging in the jungle with them, instead of sitting there, *all on his own.*

Suddenly,
he heard a **friendly voice**.
Dangling above him was
another gibbon.

"Hello, I'm Glenda!" she said, grinning.
"My friends and I are cooking jungle curry.
Are you hungry?"

Before Geoff could swallow his mouthful
of coconut juice, a warm paw grabbed him,
and he found himself swinging
hand over hand
through the trees
with his new friend.

Geoff and his new friends ate jungle curry, drank coconut juice and chit-chatted until **stars** sparkled in the sky.

After that night, Geoff and Glenda spent every moment that they could together, **laughing** and **playing** and eating bananas...

... until the day Geoff finally had to take the ferry back to the mainland.

"Goodbye, Glenda," said Geoff. "Thank you for everything."

The two gibbons gave each other one final hug, then Geoff wheeled his bike onto the ferry.

As soon as he reached the mainland, Geoff began training hard again.

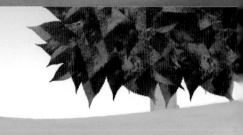

He was glued to the seat of his bike from the moment the flowers opened in the morning, until the moon shone above.

As he cycled, he imagined the moment when he'd be *whizzing* along the track...

... in a place that he'd only ever heard of before.

Finally the big day arrived.

Geoff was excited to be in Beijing, but he felt small and very lonely in the huge city filled with strangers.
"On your bikes, get set... Go!" shouted the starter.

"Come on legs, this is it!" Geoff whispered to himself.

Pedalling like mad, Geoff gradually worked his way to the front of the pack. His muscles ached and his heart pounded. Just as he was wondering whether he would make it, he heard a familiar voice cheering overhead: "Go on, Geoff, *you know you can do it!*"

Looking up, he began to grin.

Glenda, his family, and all
of the friends he had made
during his travels had come
to *support* him!

With an extra burst of speed, Geoff shot past the finish line to get...

first place!

His friends cheered and jumped up and down.

That night, there was a big jungle party with loud music and mountains of exotic fruit. Geoff and Glenda danced and chit-chatted the night away.

Then, as the sun came up they fell asleep, dreaming about their next adventure.

THE END

ABOUT THE BLACK-CRESTED GIBBON

NATURAL HABITAT: FORESTS OF SOUTHEAST ASIA, INCLUDING CHINA, VIETNAM AND LAOS

WEIGHT: UP TO 10 KG (THEY ARE ABOUT THE SIZE AND WEIGHT OF A MEDIUM SIZED DOG SUCH AS A BEAGLE)

DIET: MAINLY RIPE FRUIT, LEAF BUDS, SEEDS AND SHOOTS, OCCASIONALLY INSECTS AND EGGS

LIFESPAN: ABOUT 30 YEARS

© Terry Whittaker/ www.flpa-images.co.uk

DID YOU KNOW?

- THE BLACK-CRESTED GIBBON GETS ITS NAME FROM THE 'CREST', OR TUFT, OF BLACK FUR ON THE TOP OF ITS HEAD. IT IS ALSO KNOWN AS THE WHITE-CHEEKED GIBBON.

- ALL BLACK-CRESTED GIBBONS HAVE BLACK FUR WHEN YOUNG, BUT WHEN THE FEMALE REACHES ADULTHOOD, ALL OF HER FUR, APART FROM THE CREST, TURNS GOLDEN. MALE ADULTS ARE ALMOST COMPLETELY BLACK WITH GOLDEN OR WHITE CHEEKS.

- GIBBONS ARE ARBOREAL – I.E. THEY SPEND MOST OF THEIR LIVES IN THE TREES, RARELY COMING DOWN TO THE FOREST FLOOR. THEY EVEN SLEEP CURLED UP ON BRANCHES OR AGAINST THE TRUNK OF A TREE.

- THEY TRAVEL MAINLY BY SWINGING ARM OVER ARM BETWEEN BRANCHES, AND CAN MOVE AS FAST AS A CAR. THEY ALSO LEAP FROM TREE TO TREE, EVEN IF THE BRANCHES ARE AS FAR AS 8 M APART!

- WHEN ON THE GROUND, THEY WALK ON THEIR HIND LEGS. THEY OFTEN WALK ALONG BRANCHES, TOO, RAISING THEIR ARMS IN THE AIR TO HELP THEM BALANCE.

- GIBBONS ARE 'LESSER APES' AND UNLIKE THEIR MONKEY COUSINS, THEY DO NOT HAVE TAILS.

- IN PROPORTION TO THEIR BODY, GIBBONS HAVE EXTRA-LONG ARMS (LONGER THAN THEIR HIND LEGS).

- BLACK-CRESTED GIBBONS NORMALLY LIVE IN SMALL FAMILY GROUPS – WITH ONLY ONE ADULT MALE. THEY COMMUNICATE BY HOOTING VERY LOUDLY. THEIR MORNING 'SONG' CAN OFTEN BE HEARD ECHOING THROUGH THE FOREST FROM A DISTANCE OF ABOUT 1 KM AWAY.

- THIS SPECIES OF GIBBON IS HIGHLY ENDANGERED. IT IS THREATENED BY THE LOSS OF ITS HABITAT, AND ALSO BECAUSE IT IS HUNTED BY MAN.

ABOUT THE OLYMPIC GAMES

Fast Facts!

- The **Summer Olympic Games** are held every four years. They are followed immediately afterwards by the **Paralympic Games** – a sporting event for disabled athletes.

- The **Winter Olympics** – where participants compete in winter sports such as skiing – is held two years after the Summer Olympics. The next Winter Olympics will be held in 2010 in Vancouver, Canada.

- The Olympic Games have a long history – they were first held in Olympia, in Ancient Greece, **more than 2,700 years ago!** These games, which are known as the Ancient Olympics, were held every four years.

- The first of the modern Olympic Games took place in 1896 in **Athens, Greece**. Only 241 athletes from fourteen countries took part in those Games.

- Since then, the Olympic Games have become **the largest sporting event in the world**. At the 2004 Athens Summer Olympics, 10,500 athletes from over 200 nations took part in 301 different events ... and around 3.9 billion people watched them on television!

- The **2008 Beijing Summer Olympics** is expected to have more competitors than ever before! Beijing has prepared for the Olympics by building a huge new stadium, nicknamed the **'Bird's Nest'** because of its criss-crossed walls of steel. They have also built the futuristic National Swimming Centre, nicknamed the **'Water Cube'** because it looks like it is made out of bubbles!

Did you know?

- The **'Olympic Torch'** is lit months before the start of the Games at a special ceremony in Olympia, Greece. From there, it is carried in a special 'Torch Relay' by a series of runners, who carry the lit torch around the world, ending up in the Olympic stadium. There, the torch is used to light the Flame, which will be kept burning until the end of the Games.

- **Lucky 8!** The 2008 Beijing opening ceremony is scheduled to begin at eight minutes and eight seconds past eight in the evening, on the eighth of August (the eighth month), 2008. In other words, at **8.08.08 pm on 8.08.08!** The date and time were specially chosen because eight is considered a lucky number in China, as it sounds like the words for 'prosper' and 'wealth'!